BIRTHDAY GIRL

HARUKI MURAKAMI

BIRTHDAY GIRL

*Translated from the Japanese
by Jay Rubin*

Harvill *Secker*

LONDON

1 3 5 7 9 10 8 6 4 2

Harvill Secker, an imprint of Vintage,
20 Vauxhall Bridge Road,
London SW1V 2SA

Harvill Secker is part of the Penguin Random House group
of companies whose addresses can be found at
global.penguinrandomhouse.com

Penguin
Random House
UK

First published by Harvill Secker in 2019

'Birthday Girl' originally appeared in English in *Harper's* in 2003 and was
first published by The Harvill Press in 2004 in the short story collection
Birthday Stories, which was first published in Japanese in 2002 with the title
Bāsudei sutōrīzu by Chuokoron-Shinsha, Inc., Tokyo.

A CIP catalogue record for this book is available from the British Library

penguin.co.uk/vintage

ISBN 9781787301252

Typeset in 12.75/18.5 New Caledonia
by Integra Software Services Pvt. Ltd, Pondicherry

Printed and bound in Great Britain by Clays Ltd, Elcograf S.p.A.

Penguin Random House is committed to a sustainable future
for our business, our readers and our planet. This book is made
from Forest Stewardship Council® certified paper.

MIX
Paper from
responsible sources
FSC® C018179
www.fsc.org

BIRTHDAY GIRL

She waited on tables as usual that day, her twentieth birthday. She always worked on Fridays, but if things had gone according to plan that particular Friday, she would have had the night off. The other part-time girl had agreed to switch shifts with her as a matter of course: being screamed at by an angry chef while lugging pumpkin gnocchi and seafood *fritto misto* to customers' tables was no way to spend one's twentieth birthday. But the other girl had aggravated a cold and gone to bed with unstoppable diarrhoea and a fever of 104°, so she ended up working after all at short notice.

She found herself trying to comfort the sick girl, who had called to apologise. 'Don't worry about it,' she said. 'I wasn't going to do anything special anyway, even if it is my twentieth birthday.'

And in fact she was not all that disappointed. One reason was the terrible argument she had had a few days earlier with the boyfriend who was supposed to be with her that night. They had been going together since school. The argument had started from nothing much, but it had taken an unexpected turn for the worse until it became a long and bitter shouting match – one bad enough, she was pretty sure, to have snapped their long-standing ties once and for all. Something inside her had turned rock hard and died. He had not called her since the blow-up, and she was not going to call him.

Her workplace was one of the better-known Italian restaurants in the chic Roppongi district of Tokyo. It had been in business since the late sixties, and while its cuisine was hardly cutting edge, its high reputation was fully justified. It had many regular customers and they were never disappointed. The dining room had a calm, relaxed atmosphere without a hint of pushiness. Rather than a young crowd, the restaurant drew an older clientele that included some famous stage people and writers.

The two full-time waiters worked six days a week. She and the other part-time waitress were students who took turns working three days each. In addition there was one floor manager and, at the desk, a skinny middle-aged woman who supposedly had been there since the restaurant opened – literally sitting in the one place, it seemed, like some gloomy old character from *Little Dorrit*. She had exactly two functions: to accept payment from the customers and to answer the phone. She spoke only when necessary and always wore the same black dress. There was something cold and hard about her: if you set her afloat on the night-time sea, she would probably sink any boat that happened to ram her.

The floor manager was perhaps in his late forties. Tall and broad-shouldered, his build suggested that he had been a sportsman in his youth, but excess flesh was now beginning to accumulate on his belly and chin. His short, stiff hair was thinning at the crown, and a special ageing bachelor smell clung to him – like newsprint that had been stored in a drawer with cough drops. She had a bachelor uncle who smelled like that.

The manager always wore a black suit, white shirt, and bow tie – not a clip-on bow tie, but the real thing, tied by hand.

It was a point of pride for him that he could tie it perfectly without looking in the mirror. He performed his duties adroitly day after day. They consisted of checking the arrival and departure of guests, keeping abreast of the reservation schedule, knowing the names of regular customers, greeting them with a smile, lending a respectful ear to any complaints that might arise, giving expert advice on wines, and overseeing the work of the waiters and the waitresses. It was also his special task to deliver dinner to the room of the restaurant's owner.

*

'The owner had his own room on the sixth floor of the same building where the restaurant was,' she said. 'An apartment, or office or something.'

Somehow she and I had got on to the subject of our twentieth birthdays – what sort of day it had been for each of us. Most people remember the day they turned twenty. Hers had happened more than ten years earlier.

'He never, ever showed his face in the restaurant, though. The only one who saw him was the manager. It was strictly *his* job to deliver the owner's dinner to him. None of the other employees knew what he looked like.'

'So basically, the owner was getting home delivery from his own restaurant.'

'Correct,' she said. 'Every night at eight, the manager had to bring dinner to the owner's room. It was the restaurant's busiest time, so having the manager disappear just then was always a problem for us, but there was no way around it because that was the way it had always been done. They'd load the dinner on to one of those carts that hotels use for room service, the manager would push it into the lift wearing a respectful look on his face, and fifteen minutes later he'd come back empty-handed. Then, an hour later, he'd go up again and bring down the cart with empty plates and glasses. Every day, like clockwork. I thought it was really odd the first time I saw it happen. It was like some kind of religious ritual, you know? But after a while I got used to it, and never gave it another second thought.'

*

The owner always had chicken. The recipe and the vegetable sides were a little different every day, but the main dish was always chicken. A young chef once told her that he had tried sending up the same exact roast chicken every day for a week just to see what would happen, but there was never any complaint. A chef wants to try different ways of preparing things, of course, and each new chef would challenge himself with every technique for chicken that he could think of. They'd make elegant sauces, they'd try chickens from different suppliers, but none of their efforts had any effect: they might just as well have been throwing pebbles into an empty cave. In the end, every one of them gave up and sent the owner some run-of-the-mill chicken dish every day. That's all that was ever asked of them.

Work started as usual on her twentieth birthday, 17 November. It had been raining on and off since the afternoon, and pouring since early evening. At five o'clock the manager gathered the employees together to explain the day's specials. Servers were required to memorise them word for word and not use crib sheets: veal Milanese, pasta topped with sardines and cabbage, chestnut mousse. Sometimes the manager would play the role of a customer and test them with questions. Then came the employees' meal: waiters in *this* restaurant were not going to have growling stomachs as they took their customers' orders!

The restaurant opened its doors at six o'clock, but guests were slow to arrive because of the downpour, and several reservations were simply cancelled. Women didn't want their dresses ruined by the rain. The manager walked around tight-lipped, and the waiters killed time polishing the salt and pepper shakers or chatting with the chef about cooking. She surveyed the dining room with just one couple having their dinner and listened to the harpsichord music flowing discreetly from ceiling speakers. A deep smell of late-autumn rain worked its way from the street.

It was after seven thirty when the manager started feeling sick. He stumbled over to a chair and sat there for a while, pressing his stomach, as if he had just been shot. A greasy sweat clung to his forehead. 'I think I'd better go to the hospital,' he muttered. For him to be taken ill was a wholly uncommon occurrence: he had never missed a day since he started working in the restaurant more than ten years earlier. It was another point of pride for him that he had never been out with illness or injury, but his painful grimace made it clear that he was in a very bad way.

She stepped outside with an umbrella and hailed a taxi. One of the waiters held the manager steady and climbed into the car with him to take him to a nearby hospital. Before ducking into the cab, the manager said to her hoarsely, 'I want you to take a dinner up to room 604 at eight o'clock. All you have to do is ring the bell, say, "Your dinner is here," and leave it.'

'That's room 604, right?' she said.

'At eight o'clock,' he repeated. 'On the dot.' He grimaced again, climbed in, and the taxi took him away.

*

The rain showed no signs of letting up after the manager had left, and customers arrived at long intervals. No more than one or two tables were occupied at any time, so if the manager and one waiter had to be absent, this was a good time for it to happen. Things could get so busy that it was not unusual even for the full staff to have trouble coping.

When the owner's meal was ready at eight o'clock, she pushed the room-service trolley into the lift and rode up to the sixth floor. It was the standard meal for him: a half-bottle of red wine with the cork loosened, a thermal pot of coffee, a chicken entrée with steamed vegetables, rolls and butter. The heavy aroma of cooked chicken quickly filled the small lift. It mingled with the smell of the rain. Water droplets dotted the lift floor, suggesting that someone with a wet umbrella had recently been aboard.

She pushed the trolley down the corridor, bringing it to a stop in front of the door marked '604'. She double-checked her memory: 604. That was it. She cleared her throat and pressed the doorbell.

There was no answer. She stood there for a good twenty seconds. Just as she was thinking of pressing the bell again, the door opened inward and a skinny old man appeared. He was shorter than she was, by some four or five inches. He had on a dark suit and a tie. Against his white shirt, the tie stood out distinctly, its brownish-yellow colouring not unlike withered leaves. He made a very clean impression, his clothes perfectly pressed, his white hair smoothed down: he looked as though he were about to go out for the night to some sort of gathering. The deep wrinkles that creased his brow made her think of ravines in an aerial photograph.

'Your dinner, sir,' she said in a husky voice, then quietly cleared her throat again. Her voice grew husky whenever she was tense.

'Dinner?'

'Yes, sir. The manager took sick suddenly. I had to take his place today. Your meal, sir.'

'Oh, I see,' the old man said, almost as if talking to himself, his hand still perched on the doorknob. 'Took sick, eh? You don't say.'

'His stomach started to hurt him all of a sudden. He went to the hospital. He thinks he might have appendicitis.'

'Oh, that's not good,' the old man said, running his fingers along the wrinkles of his forehead. 'Not good at all.'

She cleared her throat again. 'Shall I bring your meal in, sir?' she asked.

'Ah yes, of course,' the old man said. 'Yes, of course, if you wish. That's fine with me.'

If I wish? she thought. What a strange way to put it. What am I supposed to wish?

The old man opened the door the rest of the way, and she wheeled the trolley inside. The floor had short grey carpeting with no area for removing shoes. The first room was a large study, as though the

apartment was more a workplace than a
residence. The window looked out on to
the nearby Tokyo Tower, its steel skeleton
outlined in lights. A large desk stood by
the window, and beside the desk was a
compact sofa and love seat. The old man
pointed to the plastic laminate coffee table
in front of the sofa. She arranged his meal
on the table: white napkin and silverware,
coffee pot and cup, wine and wine glass,
bread and butter, and the plate of chicken
and vegetables.

'If you would be kind enough to set the
dishes in the hall as usual, sir, I'll come to
get them in an hour.'

Her words seemed to snap him out of an
appreciative contemplation of his dinner.

'Oh yes, of course. I'll put them in the hall.
On the trolley. In an hour. If you wish.'

Yes, she replied inwardly, for the
moment that is exactly what I wish. 'Is
there anything else I can do for you, sir?'

'No, I don't think so,' he said after a
moment's consideration. He was wearing
black shoes polished to a high sheen. They
were small and chic. He's a stylish dresser,
she thought. And he stands very straight
for his age.

'Well, then, sir, I'll be getting back to
work.'

'No, wait just a moment,' he said.

'Sir?'

'Do you think it might be possible for
you to give me five minutes of your time,

miss? I have something I'd like to say to you.'

He was so polite in his request that it made her blush. 'I … think it should be alright,' she said. 'I mean, if it really is just five minutes.' He was her employer, after all. He was paying her by the hour. It was not a question of her giving or his taking her time. And this old man did not look like a person who would do anything bad to her.

'By the way, how old are you?' the old man asked, standing by the table with arms folded and looking directly into her eyes.

'I'm twenty now,' she said.

'Twenty *now*,' he repeated, narrowing his eyes as if peering through some kind of crack. 'Twenty *now*. As of when?'

'Well, I just turned twenty,' she said. After a moment's hesitation, she added, 'Today is my birthday, sir.'

'I *see*,' he said, rubbing his chin as if this explained a great deal for him. 'Today, is it? Today is your twentieth birthday?'

She nodded.

'Your life in this world began exactly twenty years ago today.'

'Yes, sir,' she said, 'that is so.'

'I see, I see,' he said. 'That's wonderful. Well, then, happy birthday.'

'Thank you very much,' she said, and then it dawned on her that this was the very first time all day that anyone had wished her a happy birthday. Of course, if her parents had called from Oita, she might find a message from them on her answering machine when she got home from work.

'Well, well, this is certainly a cause for celebration,' he said. 'How about a little toast? We can drink this red wine.'

'Thank you, sir, but I couldn't. I'm working now.'

'Oh, what's the harm in a little sip? No one's going to blame you if I say it's alright. Just a token drink to celebrate.'

The old man slid the cork from the bottle and dribbled a little wine into his glass for her. Then he took an ordinary drinking glass from a glass-doored cabinet and poured some wine for himself.

'Happy birthday,' he said. 'May you live a rich and fruitful life, and may there be nothing to cast dark shadows on it.'

They clinked glasses.

May there be nothing to cast dark shadows on it: she silently repeated his remark to herself. Why had he chosen such unusual words for her birthday toast?

'Your twentieth birthday comes only once in a lifetime, young lady. It's an irreplaceable day.'

'Yes, sir, I know,' she said, taking one cautious sip of wine.

'And here, on your special day, you have taken the trouble to deliver my dinner to me like a kind-hearted fairy.'

'Just doing my job, sir.'

'But still,' the old man said with a few quick shakes of the head. 'But still, lovely young miss.'

The old man sat down in the leather chair by his desk and motioned her to the sofa. She lowered herself gingerly on to the edge of the seat, with the wine glass still in her hand. Knees aligned, she tugged at her skirt, clearing her throat again. She saw raindrops tracing lines down the window pane. The room was strangely quiet.

'Today just happens to be your twentieth birthday, and on top of that you have brought me this wonderful warm meal,' the old man said as if reconfirming the situation. Then he set his glass on the desktop with a little thump. 'This has to be some kind of special convergence, don't you think?'

Not quite convinced, she managed a nod.

'Which is why,' he said, touching the knot of his withered-leaf-coloured necktie, 'I feel it is important for me to give you a birthday present. A special birthday calls for a special commemorative gift.'

Flustered, she shook her head and said, 'No, please, sir, don't give it a second thought. All I did was bring your meal the way they ordered me to.'

The old man raised both hands, palms towards her. 'No, miss, don't *you* give it a second thought. The kind of "present" I have in mind is not something tangible, not something with a price tag. To put it simply –' he placed his hands on the desk and took one long, slow breath – 'what I would like to do for a lovely young fairy such as you is to grant a wish you might have, to make your wish come true. Anything. Anything at all that you wish for – assuming that you *do* have such a wish.'

'A wish?' she asked, her throat dry.

'Something you would like to have happen, miss. If you have a wish – one wish, I'll make it come true. That is the kind of birthday present I can give you. But you had better think about it very carefully because I can grant you only one.' He raised a finger. 'Just one. You can't change your mind afterwards and take it back.'

She was at a loss for words. One wish? Whipped by the wind, raindrops tapped unevenly at the window pane. As long as she remained silent, the old man looked into her eyes, saying nothing. Time marked its irregular pulse in her ears.

'I have to wish for something, and it will be granted?'

Instead of answering her question, the old man – hands still side by side on the desk – just smiled. He did it in the most natural and amiable way.

'Do you *have* a wish, miss – or not?' he asked gently.

*

'This really did happen,' she said, looking straight at me. 'I'm not making it up.'

'Of course not,' I said. She was not the sort of person to invent some goofy story out of thin air. 'So ... did you make a wish?'

She went on looking at me for a while, then released a tiny sigh. 'Don't get me wrong,' she said. 'I wasn't taking him one hundred per cent seriously myself. I mean, at twenty you're not exactly living in a fairy-tale world any more. If this was his idea of a joke, though, I had to hand it to him for coming up with it on the spot. He was a dapper old fellow with a twinkle in his eye, so I decided to play along with him. It *was* my twentieth birthday, after all: I reckoned I ought to have *something* not-so-ordinary happen to me that day. It wasn't a question of believing or not believing.'

I nodded without saying anything.

'You can understand how I felt, I'm sure. My twentieth birthday was coming to an end without anything special happening, nobody wishing me a happy birthday, and all I'm doing is carrying tortellini with anchovy sauce to people's tables.'

I nodded again. 'Don't worry,' I said. 'I understand.'

'So I made a wish.'

*

The old man kept his gaze fixed on her, saying nothing, hands still on the desk.

Also on the desk were several thick folders that might have been account books, plus writing implements, a calendar and a lamp with a green shade. Lying among them, his small hands looked like another set of desktop furnishings. The rain continued to beat against the window, the lights of Tokyo Tower filtering through the shattered drops.

The wrinkles on the old man's forehead deepened slightly. 'That is your wish?'

'Yes,' she said. 'That is my wish.'

'A bit unusual for a girl your age,' he said. 'I was expecting something different.'

'If it's no good, I'll wish for something else,' she said, clearing her throat. 'I don't mind. I'll think of something else.'

'No, no,' the old man said, raising his hands and waving them like flags. 'There's nothing wrong with it, not at all. It's just a little surprising, miss. Don't you have something else? For example, you want to be prettier, or smarter, or rich: you're OK with not wishing for something like that – something an ordinary girl would ask for?'

She took some moments to search for the right words. The old man just waited, saying nothing, his hands at rest together on the desk again.

'Of course I'd like to be prettier or smarter or rich. But I really can't imagine what would happen to me if any of those things came true. They might be more than I could handle. I still don't really know what life is all about. I don't know how it *works.*'

'I see,' the old man said, intertwining his fingers and separating them again. 'I see.'

'So, is my wish OK?'

'Of course,' he said. 'Of course. It's no trouble at all for me.'

The old man suddenly fixed his eyes on a spot in the air. The wrinkles of his forehead deepened: they might have been the wrinkles of his brain itself as it concentrated on his thoughts. He seemed to be staring at something – perhaps all-but-invisible bits of down – floating in the air. He opened his arms wide, lifted himself slightly from his chair, and whipped his palms together with a dry smack. Settling in the chair again, he slowly ran his fingertips along the wrinkles of his brow as if to soften them, and then turned to her with a gentle smile.

'That did it,' he said. 'Your wish has been granted.'

'Already?'

'Yes, it was no trouble at all. Your wish has been granted, lovely miss. Happy birthday. You may go back to work now. Don't worry, I'll put the trolley in the hall.'

She took the lift down to the restaurant. Empty-handed now, she felt almost disturbingly light, as though she were walking on some sort of mysterious fluff.

'Are you OK? You look spaced out,' the younger waiter said to her.

She gave him an ambiguous smile and shook her head. 'Oh, really? No, I'm fine.'

'Tell me about the owner. What's he like?'

'I dunno, I didn't get a very good look at him,' she said, cutting the conversation short.

An hour later she went to bring the trolley down. It was out in the corridor, utensils in place. She lifted the lid to find the chicken and vegetables gone. The wine bottle and coffee pot were empty. The door to room 604 stood there, closed and expressionless. She stared at it for a time, feeling it might open at any moment, but it did not open. She brought the trolley down in the lift and wheeled it in to the dishwasher. The chef looked blankly at the plate: empty as always.

*

'I never saw the owner again,' she said. 'Not once. The manager turned out to have just an ordinary stomach ache and went back to delivering the owner's meal again himself the next day. I left the job after New Year's, and I've never been back to the place. I don't know, I just felt it was better not to go near there, kind of like a premonition.'

She toyed with a paper coaster, thinking her own thoughts. 'Sometimes I get the feeling that everything that happened to me on my twentieth birthday was some sort of illusion. It's as though something happened to make me think that things happened that never really happened at all. But I know for sure that they *did* happen. I can still bring back vivid images of every piece of furniture and every knick-knack in room 604. What happened to me in there really happened, and it had an important meaning for me, too.'

The two of us kept silent, drinking our drinks and thinking our separate thoughts.

'Do you mind if I ask you one thing?' I asked. 'Or, more precisely, *two* things.'

'Go ahead,' she said. 'I imagine you're going to ask me what I wished for that time. That's the first thing you want to know.'

'But it looks as though you don't want to talk about that.'

'Does it?'

I nodded.

She put the coaster down and narrowed her eyes as if staring at something in the distance. 'You're not supposed to tell anybody what you wished for, you know.'

'I won't try to drag it out of you,' I said. 'I *would* like to know whether or not it came true, though. And also – whatever the wish itself might have been – whether or not you later came to regret what it was you chose to wish for. Were you ever sorry you didn't wish for something else?'

'The answer to the first question is yes and also no. I still have a lot of living left to do, probably. I haven't seen how things are going to work out to the end.'

'So it was a wish that takes time to come true?'

'You could say that. Time is going to play an important role.'

'Like in cooking certain dishes?'

She nodded.

I thought about that for a moment, but the only thing that came to mind was the image of a gigantic pie cooking slowly in an oven at low heat.

'And the answer to my second question?'

'What was that again?'

'Whether you ever regretted your choice of what to wish for.'

A moment of silence followed. The eyes she turned on me seemed to lack any depth. The desiccated shadow of a smile flickered at the corners of her mouth, suggesting a kind of hushed sense of resignation.

'I'm married now,' she said. 'To a CPA three years older than me. And I have two children, a boy and a girl. We have an Irish setter. I drive an Audi, and I play tennis with my girlfriends twice a week. That's the life I'm living now.'

'Sounds pretty good to me,' I said.

'Even if the Audi's bumper has two dents?'

'Hey, bumpers are *made* for denting.'

'That would make a great bumper sticker,' she said. '"Bumpers are for denting."'

I looked at her mouth when she said that.

'What I'm trying to tell you is this,' she said more softly, scratching an earlobe. It was a beautifully shaped earlobe. 'No matter what they wish for, no matter how far they go, people can never be anything but themselves. That's all.'

'There's another good bumper sticker,' I said. '"No matter how far they go, people can never be anything but themselves."'

She laughed aloud, with a real show of pleasure, and the shadow was gone.

She rested her elbow on the bar and looked at me. 'Tell me,' she said. 'What would you have wished for if you had been in my position?'

'On the night of my twentieth birthday, you mean?'

'Uh-huh.'

I took some time to think about that, but I couldn't come up with a single wish.

'I can't think of anything,' I confessed. 'I'm too far away now from my twentieth birthday.'

'You really can't think of anything?'

I nodded.

'Not one thing?'

'Not one thing.'

She looked into my eyes again – straight in – and said, 'That's because you've already *made* your wish.'

*

'But you had better think about it very carefully, my lovely young fairy, because I can grant you only one.' In the darkness somewhere, an old man wearing a withered-leaf-coloured tie raises a finger. 'Just one. You can't change your mind afterwards and take it back.'